DADDY GOES TO MEETINGS

Johanna O'Flaherty and Hortensia DeJesus

Illustrated by Lina Safar

CRP®

CENTRAL RECOVERY PRESS

LAS VEGAS

We love our daddy, and our daddy loves us. He does lots of fun things with us like reading books and riding bikes and playing on swings.

We love our mommy, and our mommy loves us. She does lots of fun things with us like baking cookies and painting pictures and playing spelling games.

We love being with our daddy and mommy. We do lots of fun things together like going on picnics and watching movies and playing hide-and-seek.

But there was a time when our daddy wasn't so fun to be around. Sometimes he looked mad and sometimes he looked sad. And sometimes he wouldn't leave the bathroom till Mommy brought him a fizzy drink.

Sometimes Daddy didn't say very much
and sometimes he shouted at Mommy.

Sometimes Daddy wouldn't come home for dinner.
And we wondered if it was our fault that Daddy stayed away.

Sometimes when Daddy got really mad, Mommy would take us to Grandma's and Grandpa's house to stay for a while.

Then one day, some of Daddy's friends knocked on our door.
They came to see him because they heard he was sick.

They told us they knew how
to help our daddy. His friends
stayed with him until he could
get out of bed. We were so
happy his friends came to help.

Daddy's friends took him to
meet some people even though
he didn't think it would help.

It was at this meeting
that Daddy found a lot
of people like him.

Daddy went to a meeting a day for a while.
Sometimes Mommy would drive us to meet him after the
meeting. We love seeing Daddy so happy with his friends.

Daddy still goes to meetings, and sometimes we go too, even if it's raining outside.

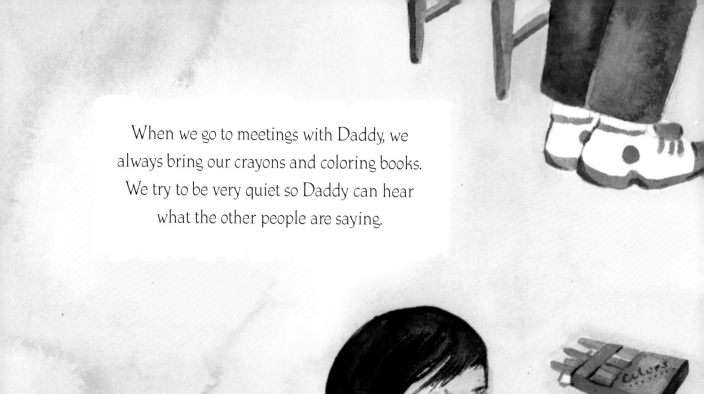

When we go to meetings with Daddy, we
always bring our crayons and coloring books.
We try to be very quiet so Daddy can hear
what the other people are saying.

We love our daddy and we are so happy
he goes to meetings. He doesn't come
home late anymore and helps
Mommy cook our dinner.

Daddy takes us to school and
helps us with homework and
sometimes watches us play.

Our daddy goes to meetings so he can stay well. We're not sure how meetings can make someone feel better, but we know that going to meetings gave us back our daddy.

The End

Talking with Children about Addiction Treatment
A GUIDE FOR PARENTS

1. Focus on the positive. Anytime it's necessary to explain a difficult situation to a child, such as when a parent starts addiction treatment, try to balance happy times with times not so happy. Even if these are simple things, it helps teach that in the best of times there are things that are not perfect and in difficult times there are things worth celebrating.

2. Keep it simple—at a child's level. When talking with more than one child, speak at the youngest level. Once everyone understands the basics, encourage questions. If there is a large age difference, talk to everyone first, and then follow up individually.

3. Be completely honest. Start with something like, "Daddy's gone to the hospital and/or meetings to get help for his alcohol (or other drug) use." Watch and listen to the child's response and answer any questions.

4. Initiate the conversation, do not wait for the child to ask about where the parent is or what has and will be happening. Putting off this important discussion only increases the child's sense of uncertainty and worry.

5. Do not lecture. Do not talk at or down to the child. Don't assume this is too complex a topic for children. Don't tell the child about what he or she *should* feel or believe. Ask about feelings, and then listen carefully to the answers. You want to present a calm presence so the child will feel safe to share whatever emotions he or she is experiencing.

6. Be helpful, try to understand the concerns, feelings, and beliefs of the child. Once you understand, offer explicit help and support. This might sound like "You've told me you are feeling _____. When I feel _____ it helps me if the people I love do_____. Would that be something you'd like? Is there something you can tell me to do that would work better for you?" Remember, all children need reassurance. Younger children often only need basic information and consistent reassurance that they are not to blame and that the absent parent loves them and will be back.

7. Share your own feelings and concerns. It's important to give a simple honest disclosure of your emotional state, but it should be framed positively and reassuringly. For example: "With Daddy gone for several weeks, I sometimes feel sad. Fortunately Grandma is helping us out and that makes things easier for me. All of your help has really meant a lot to me, too. I'm sorry if I was grumpy this morning. I don't want to take out feeling sad on you." Remember to **not** make the child your confidant. Find a twelve-step support group that you feel comfortable with to share your concerns. It is also helpful to get a sponsor as soon as possible.

8. Share your values, including that people we love are loveable even when they disappoint or inconvenience us. Communicate that addiction and mental illness are diseases like diabetes and high blood pressure that need treatment and support.

9. Be available, and do not make the "crisis" the entire focus of your lives. While you may need to eliminate some family activities, keep those important for your own self-care and support. You cannot support others or your children without first taking care of your own needs.

10. Be patient and supportive. It is common for children under stress to be extra needy and fall back on behavior they grew out of months before. If the behavior goes on too long, or seems beyond your ability, please talk with your child's primary healthcare provider. It may be a good idea to ask a family member or friend of the same sex as the absent parent to spend extra time with the child.

11. Be clear and specific about everything, including that you are available and **want** your children to talk about feelings, questions, or worries at any time. It is important you are consistent and reassuring. If you are overwhelmed and worried, settle yourself and get the support you need before starting the conversation with your child.

Important Talking Points to Remember

Neither the child nor
others in the family
caused the problem.

* * *

Neither the child nor others in
the family are able to cure the
disease, but effective treatment
is available and the parent/
family member is receiving
treatment.

* * *

Neither the child nor
others in the family can
control the disease.

The most important thing
the child and other family
members can do is take good
care of themselves.

* * *

Taking good care of yourself
always includes communicating
feelings, making healthy
choices that help you, and
celebrating who you are—
specifically your strengths and
abilities—as individuals
and as a family.

Central Recovery Press (CRP) is committed to publishing exceptional materials addressing addiction treatment, recovery, and behavioral healthcare topics, including original and quality books, audio/visual communications, and web-based new media. Through a diverse selection of titles, we seek to contribute a broad range of unique resources for professionals, recovering individuals and their families, and the general public.

For more information, visit www.centralrecoverypress.com.

Publisher: Central Recovery Press
             3321 N. Buffalo Drive
             Las Vegas, NV 89129

20 19 18 17 16 15   1 2 3 4 5

ISBN: 978-1-937612-79-5 (paper)

Cover design and illustrations by Lina Safar
Interior layout by Sara Streifel, Think Creative Design

About the Authors

Johanna O'Flaherty, PhD

Johanna O'Flaherty is the CEO of Las Vegas Recovery Center (LVRC) and is an experienced executive with over twenty-five years of national and international experience providing leadership, program development, vision, and direction to interdisciplinary teams around the globe. She has special expertise in chemical dependency and emergency response. She is a Nationally Certified Addiction Counselor and is a Certified Employee Assistance Professional. Most recently, she was Vice President of Treatment Services at the Betty Ford Center where she was responsible for clinical program development and monitoring the efficacy of new tracks. Dr. O'Flaherty was the Clinical Program Director at Sierra Tucson and oversaw all aspects of the Sierra Tucson Program, including recruiting personnel and maintaining appropriate staffing levels. She was Director of Special Health Services and the Trauma Response Team Coordinator for Trans World Airlines from 1992 to 2005.

Hortensia DeJesus, CADC

Hortensia DeJesus is the Family Services Manager for Las Vegas Recovery Center (LVRC). Ms. DeJesus has been with the company since November of 2006 and has more than four years experience within the addiction treatment and recovery fields. She currently manages LVRC's Family Renewal Program, which includes a specially designed Family Renewal Weekend and Family Support Group that meets once a week. The Family Renewal Program recognizes that family participation, education, and recovery are vital to the successful outcome of long-term sustained recovery and change for the addict.

About the Illustrator

Lina Safar

Lina Safar grew up in Kiev, Ukraine, and has lived most of her life in Syria. She graduated in 2004 with honors from the University of Damascus School of Fine Arts with a BA in Visual Communications and Illustration.

While still studying she began working in design, painting, and book illustration and has participated in many local and international exhibitions. Lina's inspiration comes from everyday life and her travels inside and outside her own head.

Lina has illustrated over fifteen books for international and American writers.

She currently lives in the US.

Also Available from CRP for Young Readers

Mommy's Gone to Treatment

Denise D. Crosson, PhD · Illustrated by Mike Motz
$14.95 US · ISBN: 978-0-9799869-1-8 (paper)

Mommy's Coming Home from Treatment

Denise D. Crosson, PhD · Illustrated by Mike Motz
$14.95 US · ISBN: 978-0-9799869-4-9 (paper)

First Star I See

Jaye Andras Caffrey · Illustrated by Lynne Adamson
$12.95 US · ISBN: 978-1-936290-01-7 (paper) · ISBN: 978-1-936290-48-2 (e-book)

The Secret of Willow Ridge

Helen H. Moore · Illustrated by John Blackford
$12.95 US · ISBN: 978-0-9818482-0-4 (paper) · ISBN: 978-1-936290-38-3 (e-book)

Why Is Brian So Fat?

Gary Solomon, PhD · Illustrated by Lynne Adamson
$14.95 US · ISBN: 978-1-936290-74-1 (paper) · ISBN: 978-1-936290-76-5 (e-book)